Child Care Grant   9/02   # 7.50

Short "i"
and Long "i"
Play a Game

The Child's World®

Library of Congress Cataloging-in-Publication Data
Moncure, Jane Belk.
Short "i" and long "i" play a game / by Jane Belk Moncure ;
illustrated by Norman Young.
p. cm.
Summary: A brief story in which characters representing the short "i"
sound and the long "i" sound look for these vowels in different words.
ISBN 1-56766-930-1 (lib. bdg.)
[1. English language—Vowels—Fiction.]   I. Young, N. (Norman), ill. II. Title.
PZ7.M739 Sgi 2001
[E]—dc21
00-010850

Short "i"
and Long "i"
Play a Game

Jane Belk Moncure
illustrated by Norman Young

This is  . She has a special sound.

 Igloo begins with her short "i" sound.

So does 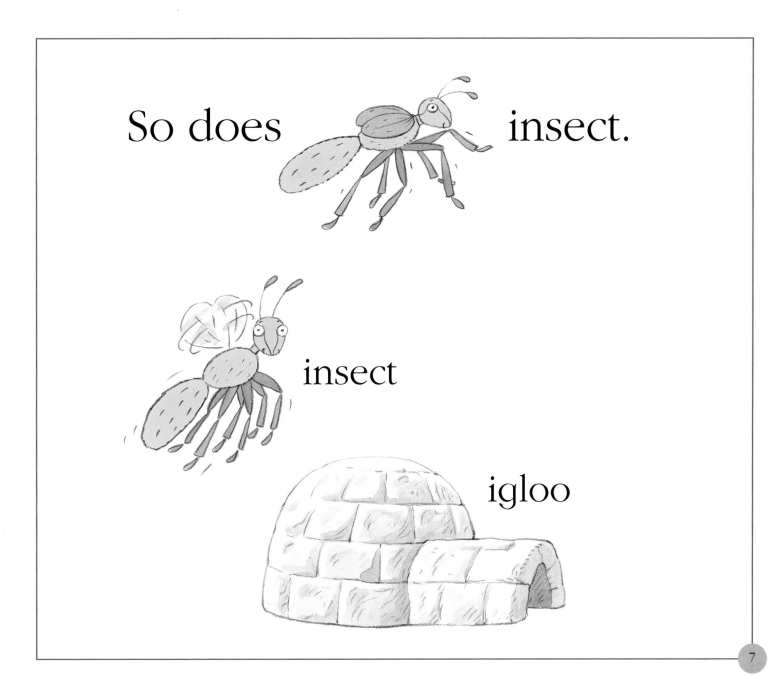 insect.

insect

igloo

This is  . He has a different sound.

Ice begins with his long "i" sound.

So does icicle.

Can you hear the short **i**
and the long **i** sounds?

9

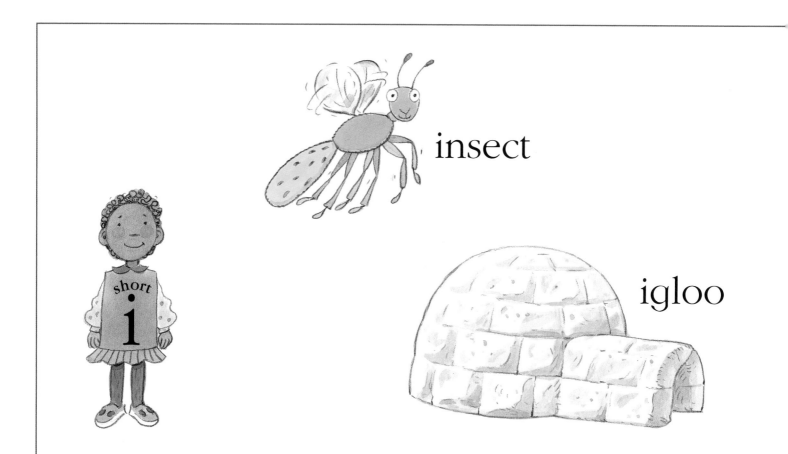

insect

igloo

One day, Short "i" said,
"Let's play a game. I will look
for my sound in words.

icicle

long
i

ice

You can look for your sound
in words. We'll see who can
find the most words."

I found inchworms…

many, many inchworms.

Then she found iguanas…
many, many iguanas.

"I will win!" she said.

Long i found

an iris

and
an island.

He also found

an iceberg.

"No! I will win!" he said.

iris

icicle

iceberg

island

ice

Long "i" counted. "I win," he said. "I have the most words."

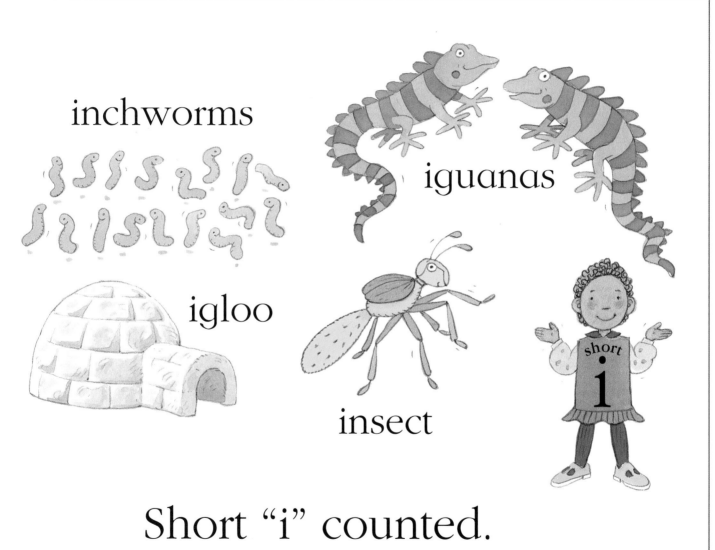

inchworms

iguanas

igloo

insect

short i

Short "i" counted.
"No! No! No!" she said.

"I will use my eyes

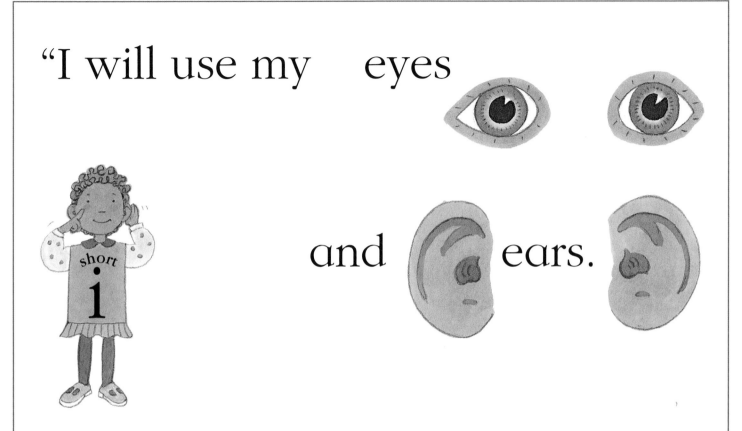

and ears.

My sound hides in words.
I will find words with my
sound in the middle of them."

found

a pig

and a fish.

Then she found a ship...

and a

hippo.

"Now I will win!" said .

"No! No! No!" said Long "i."

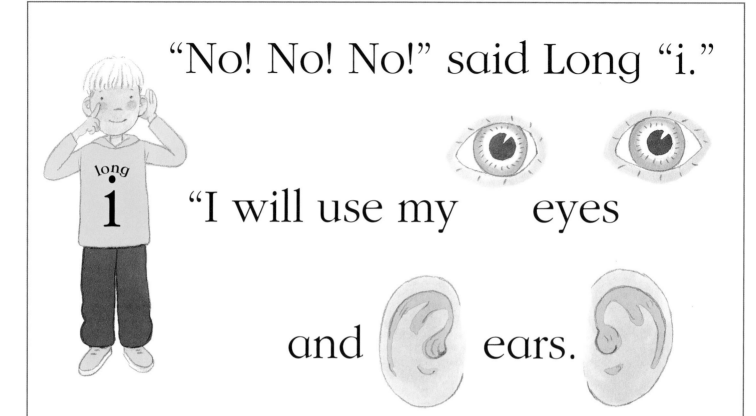

"I will use my eyes

and ears.

My sound hides in words, too.
I will find words with my sound
in the middle of them."

Long **i** found

a kite

and a bike.

Then he found a pipe,

a dime,

and a dinosaur.

"My! My!" said **long i**. "I will surely win!"

igloo

insect

iguanas

hippo

inchworms

pig

short
i

ship

fish

Can you tell who won?

icicle

ice

iris

iceberg

dinosaur

island

pipe

dime

kite

bike

long i

Can you read more words with 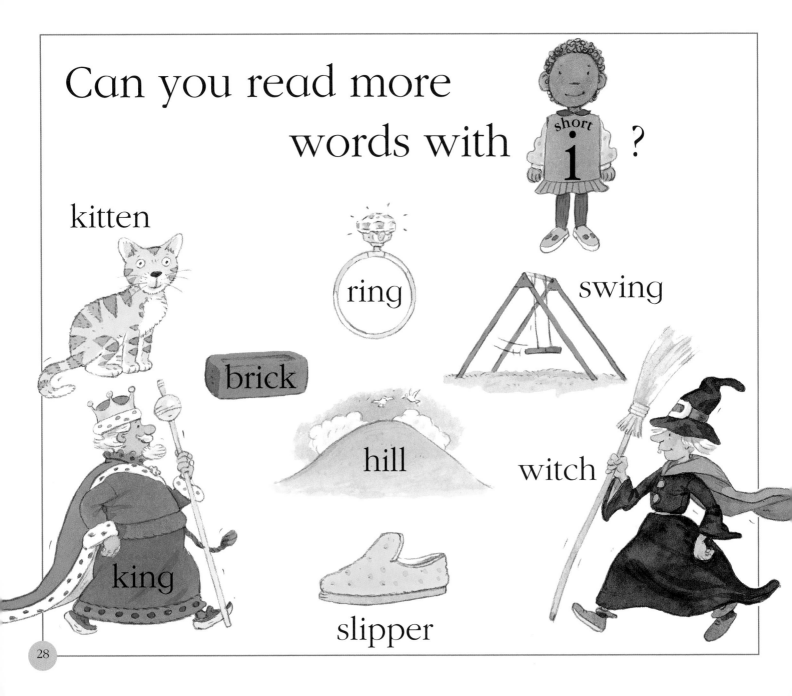 ?

kitten

ring

swing

brick

hill

witch

king

slipper

Can you read more words with  long i ?

pie

smile

ivy

tie

lion

hive

iron

spider

29

Now you make up a game!

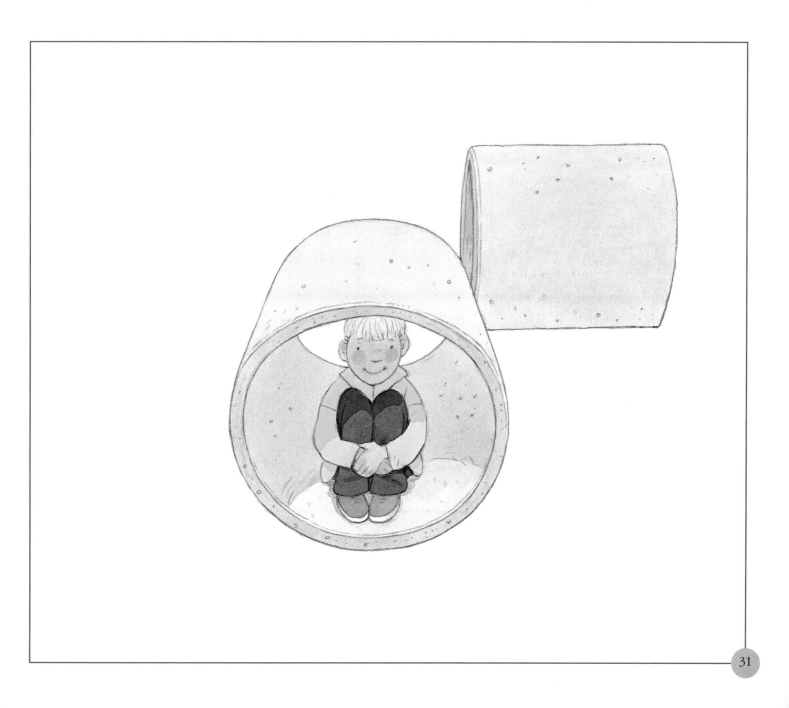

ABOUT THE AUTHOR AND ILLUSTRATOR

Jane Belk Moncure began her writing career when she was in kindergarten. She has never stopped writing. Many of her children's stories and poems have been published, to the delight of young readers, including her son Jim, whose childhood experiences found their way into many of her books.

Mrs. Moncure's writing is based upon an active career in early childhood education. A recipient of an M.A. degree from Columbia University, Mrs. Moncure has taught and directed nursery, kindergarten, and primary grade programs in California, New York, Virginia, and North Carolina. As a former member of the faculties of Virginia Commonwealth University and the University of Richmond, she taught prospective teachers in early childhood education.

Mrs. Moncure has travelled extensively abroad, studying early childhood programs in the United Kingdom, The Netherlands, and Switzerland. She was the first president of the Virginia Association for Early Childhood Education and received its award for outstanding service to young children. A resident of North Carolina, Mrs. Moncure is currently a full-time writer and educational consultant. She is married to Dr. James A. Moncure, former vice president of Elon College.

Norman Young spent his childhood on a small farm nestled at the foot of the Preseli Hills in Pembrokeshire, South West Wales. He started his artistic career as a film animator in London and then in Zagreb. Eventually he settled in Devon, where he lives beside a river that runs between the moors and the sea. It was here that he started his work as an illustrator of children's books. Norman has always had a lifelong interest in history and travel. Taking a month off work each year, he visits new places either by train or by bicycle—and he never goes anywhere without his sketchbook.